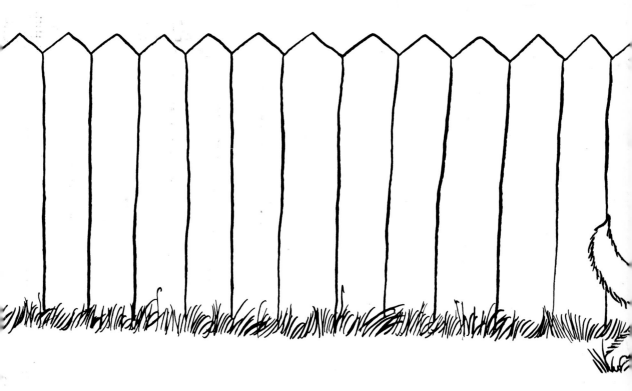

SPIKE in TROUBLE

Written and illustrated by
Paulette Bogan

G. P. Putnam's Sons
New York

G. P. Putnam's Sons, Reg. U.S. Pat. & Tm. Off.
Published simultaneously in Canada.
Manufactured in China by South China Printing Co. (1988) Ltd.
Designed by Carolyn T. Fucile. Text set in Clichee Bold.
Library of Congress Cataloging-in-Publication Data
Bogan, Paulette. Spike in trouble / by Paulette Bogan.
p. cm. Summary: Spike enjoys attending obedience school
after someone causes a lot of mischief at home,
but upon his return he exposes the real culprit.
[1. Dogs—Fiction. 2. Dogs—Training—Fiction.] I. Title.
PZ7.B6357835 Su 2003 [E]—dc21 2001048250
ISBN 0-399-23765-8
1 3 5 7 9 10 8 6 4 2
First Impression

With love and thanks to
Josephine, my friend since first grade
&
Victoria Wells, for always being there.

First SOMEONE ate one of the steaks right off the barbecue.

Then SOMEONE knocked the trash cans over.
"Spike, how could you do this?" Shannon asked.

"GRRR?" mumbled Spike.
What was Shannon talking about?

SOMEONE chewed up one of Dad's favorite boots.

"Oh, Spike, you know better than that," Dad said.
"ARF, ARF!" barked Spike. He DID know better.

Then SOMEONE dug up Mom's flower bed.

"Spike!" Mom yelled.
"YEOWZZA!" said Spike.

Spike was confused. He had not done
any of those things, but everyone was mad at him.

The next day, Spike was on his way to obedience
school. He had never been to school before.
At least Shannon was with him.

Soon Spike found out he really liked school.
He was good at almost everything.

He could walk on the leash . . .

stay when he was told . . .

shake paws . . .

roll over . . .

ALMOST get over the hurdle . . .

and of course, his specialty, fetch a Frisbee!
"WOOF WOOF!" said Spike.

Spike even made a new friend and got a blue ribbon.
"RRRUUFF!" he barked.

Shannon was so happy that Spike
was back to his good old self.

Finally school was over.
But that's when the trouble started again.

First it was the laundry—everywhere.

And then Mom's newspaper was missing.
That was the last straw.

Spike decided to find out for himself.
"GRRRRR!" growled Spike. He waited . . .

and watched . . .

and waited . . .

and finally he saw—her!
"RUFF! RUFF! RUFF!" barked Spike.

It was his new friend!
"AAARRROOO!" he howled.

Shannon ran outside.
"So you're the one causing all the trouble!"
she said to the little dog.

"I'm sorry, but unless you can behave,
you will have to go home."
The little dog looked scared. Spike felt bad.

"And I'm sorry I thought it was you, Spike,"
said Shannon.
SLURP. Spike gave Shannon a big doggy kiss.

All afternoon, Spike hoped that the little dog
would come back.

And when she did,
she brought back Mom's newspaper!